A MAXTON BOOK ABOUT

HAWAII

by Christie McFall

In collaboration with
Francis McFall

Reviewed for technical accuracy by
Eileen Teclaff, M.A.
Cambridge University
Geographical Consultant

Maxton Publishers, Inc.
New York

U. S. S. R.   ALASKA

Anchorage

Juneau

Seattle

San Francisc[o]

2395 mi.

Los Angeles

Midway Is.

To Tokyo 3850 mi.

Hawaiian Islands

To Sydney 5073 mi.

Honolulu

"Loveliest Fleet of Islands"

Hawaii is composed of a chain of islands spread out over the central Pacific for 1,600 miles and separated from the mainland by 2,000 miles of ocean. These islands are the tops of mountains which have been built up from the ocean floor by many thousands of volcanic eruptions.

As the tops of the mountains rose above the water, waves, winds and streams began to wear them away. From then on it was a battle between the volcanic eruptions and the forces of erosion. Some of the smaller islands in the chain are remnants that project only a few feet above the surface of the ocean. But even the smallest of the islands rises an average of 15,000 feet from the bottom of the sea and Mauna Kea rises over 30,000 feet from the ocean floor.

The northernmost of the main islands seem to be the oldest and have been deeply cut by erosion. Kauai has several deep

valleys. Waimea Canyon, which is over one-half mile deep, rivals the Grand Canyon. Hawaii is the southernmost island and the youngest of the islands. Here, Mauna Loa and Kilauea Volcanoes are still active so they are almost unmarred by erosion.

Plant spores and seeds, borne by currents and winds and migratory birds, eventually found their way to these once barren islands and mantled them with a carpet of vegetation.

Long before the voyages of discovery to North America, Polynesians sailed thousands of miles across the Pacific in open canoes. They carried with them many kinds of plants as well as dogs, pigs and chickens.

More than 90% of the 1,700 kinds of plants found in Hawaii when the white man arrived, grew no place else in the world. This is also true of over 90% of the 3,750 insects and 80% of the 92 species of birds.

Hawaii was isolated until the late eighteenth century. Since then many people have migrated to the islands from all over the world.

Hawaii is a land of flowers, beaches, sunshine, volcanoes and deeply cut mountains. It is a land of people of many nationalities, all living together in harmony. Often, "Hawaii" is mispronounced. It is correctly pronounced "Hah-wy-ee."

Hawaiian Islands

Mauna Kea

Coral Ledges

Mauna Kea — the world's highest mountain measured from its ocean base

Ginger — lei flower

Wood Roses
and Butterfly Fish

Tropical beauty is everywhere in Hawaii; from exotic, sweet ginger flower leis to the unique monkey-pod trees.

It takes over 100 ginger flowers for an average lei, but some flowers are always blooming in Hawaii. The pikake, a species of white jasmine, and ginger are used for some of the islands' unusual perfumes.

The monkey-pod or Ohia, one of hundreds of flowering trees, has a massive trunk with wide-reaching limbs, like the spokes of a gigantic umbrella. Native craftsmen carve bowls, platters and even tables from its hard, decorative wood.

Hats, baskets, purses and mats are woven of dried leaves from the pandanus (hala) tree. Each leaf is bent down as if it were broken by the wind.

The sausage tree looks like a display of meat in a butcher's market with its fruit hanging on in the shape of a "baloney," a foot and a half long and three or four inches wide. Palm trees are a reminder that Hawaii has a subtropical climate and the banyan, from India, also thrives here.

Night blooming Cereus

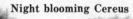

Wood rose

Banana bloom

The nene or Hawaiian goose

Famous orchids are so common that you can buy seedlings at the "dime" stores. There are over 4,000 varieties of hibiscus, the official flower of the islands. The night-blooming cereus is perhaps the most interesting flower. A mile-long hedge in Honolulu attracts many people on moonlit nights. The light brown wood roses are actually the seed-bearing parts of a vine. Florists make use of them for their wide, many-colored leaves.

Although Bird, Butterfly, Convict and Humuhumunukunukua-pua may be strange names for fish, they are actually common fish in Hawaii, purchased from commercial fishermen for display in the Honolulu aquarium. Many of these tropical fishes are found nowhere else in the world.

The nene, or Hawaiian goose, has been the official bird of Hawaii since 1957. It was once nearly extinct and is still extremely rare and protected.

Strange tropical fish found in Hawaiian waters

Philippine boy
in coconut frond hat

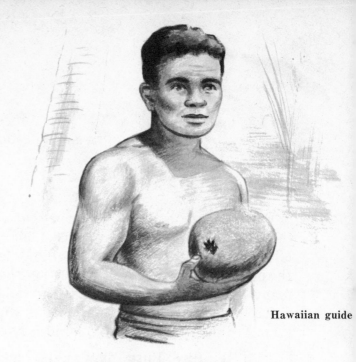

Hawaiian guide

Mother Hubbard or
muumuu style of dress

People of the World

About 1,000 years ago, Polynesians came to Hawaii in outrigger canoes from South Sea Islands. The pure-blooded Hawaiians are the descendants of these people.

The population of Hawaii dropped from the 300,000 estimated by Captain Cook after he landed in 1778, to some 82,000 Polynesian-Hawaiians by 1850. This was thought to be due to the Hawaiians having little resistance to the diseases of the white man.

Throughout the 19th century, Hawaii's productive development was handicapped by labor shortages. Hawaiian kings tried to import Chinese and natives from other Polynesian Islands to the south. After a few unsuccessful attempts, including problems with South Sea head hunters, the idea was given up.

Later, many people from many countries did come to Hawaii. Each group brought their own languages and customs. Now, almost 600,000 people live there. It was this

Ti plant

Hawaiian child
in Ti leaf skirt

Japanese girl in traditional costume

increased population that helped enlarge the sugar and pineapple industries. People of Japanese descent are the most numerous, followed by Caucasian (white), part-Hawaiian, Filipinos and Chinese. Only about 10,000 almost pure-blooded Hawaiians remain.

As the United States mainland has absorbed people from Europe, Hawaii has become America's melting pot of the Pacific. Nowhere do people of such different cultures live together in such friendship and have such equality of opportunity.

Hawaiians are a happy people whose culture has given us a distinctive music; a dance form, the hula, and the sport of surfboarding. Surfing was originally a common Hawaiian sport and also a sacred sport of kings. The origin of the hula is not known but it is said that 262 types were danced at King Kalakaua's coronation.

The Hawaiian language is quite similar to the Polynesian Island languages. It has only twelve letters, 5 vowels and 7 consonants, compared to our 26 letters. The Hawaiian native feast is the "luau" which is actually the word for the taro leaf used to wrap some of the delicious food served. The main dish is a whole pig, split, filled with hot stones, then buried in a pit with hot rocks surrounding it.

Liquid Sunshine and Double Rainbows

Weather in Hawaii is ideal. The cold California Current swings out southwestward from our Pacific coast and brings these tropical islands a cooler climate than would otherwise be expected. Light breezes blow nearly every day of the year. Severe storms are rare. Temperatures are mild, averaging about 75 degrees. There are only a few degrees difference between the summer and winter averages.

Rainfall varies greatly — from 10 inches to over 400 inches a year. The greatest extreme occurs on the island of Kauai. Here is one of the wettest spots on earth, yet only a few miles away it rains hardly at all. In general, rain is heavy on the windward side of the mountains and light on the lee side.

Very often rainfall will be so light that you can walk in it without a raincoat and not get wet. Hawaiians call this "liquid sunshine." Rainbows sometimes occur many times in a single day and double rainbows are common. In the second bow their color order is reversed.

Natives attack — Captain Cook is killed

Captain Cook Visits Hawaii

In 1778, Captain James Cook, the distinguished English navigator, first sighted the Hawaiian Islands. His ships, the Resolution and the Discovery anchored in Waimea Bay, Kauai. Cook went ashore and the natives believed him to be the Hawaiian god Lono who had returned as had been prophesied.

Cook was much impressed with their feather capes of yellow and red. He traded a few big nails for several of these gorgeous capes. They are now on display at the British museum, still as brilliant as ever. After trading with the natives, Cook sailed to Niihau where he landed again.

The following year, Cook anchored in Kealakekua Bay, on the island of Hawaii. He was again worshipped as a god and was given presents.

Quarrels developed and thefts occurred. When the large cutter of the Discovery was stolen, Cook decided to take the king prisoner until it was returned. The natives attacked and Cook was killed.

Monument to Captain Cook

Feather Cloaks and Giant Slides

The early Hawaiians were big people with golden brown skin. They had black, wavy hair, dark eyes and large features. The ruling chiefs as well as their wives sometimes weighed between 300 and 400 pounds, for size was considered a measure of their high birth. One of the sports of Hawaiian kings was coasting down the mountain sides. A long course was covered with stones, soil and slippery grass to form the giant slides.

Houses in Hawaii were made with poles stuck in the ground covered with thick thatching. They had no windows. The entrance was a hole about three feet high. The earth floor was covered with grass, pebbles or woven mats. Hawaiians ate sugar cane, bananas, sweet potatoes, coconut, taro, breadfruit

**Statue of
King Kamehameha I**

**Pageant held
during Aloha Week**

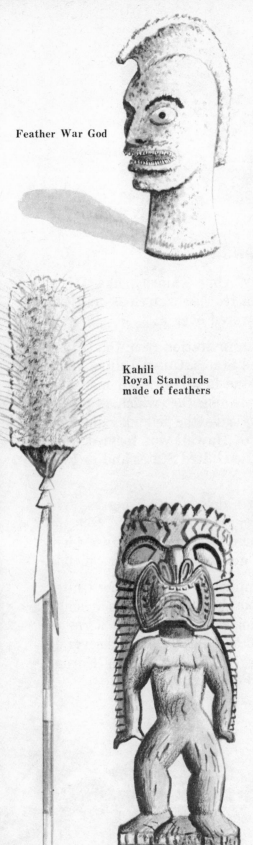

Feather War God

Kahili
Royal Standards
made of feathers

Temple Image

and plantain (similar to banana). Taro needed careful cultivation. Both the big leaves and the roots were eaten. Poi, the Hawaiian staff of life, is made from baked taro root. It is pounded and mashed with water, then allowed to ferment.

Hawaiian cloth called tapa, was made from the soaked inner bark of the paper mulberry. The pulp was then scraped from tough fibers and the fibers beaten. It was more like paper than cloth.

Captain Cook had found that the larger islands were ruled as independent kingdoms by chiefs. The greatest of these chiefs was Kamehameha I, who took over as chief of the island of Hawaii and later united other islands under his rule. On Oahu where he met and defeated the forces of the local king, many warriors were driven over the steep "pali" or cliff.

Occasional ships visited the islands. Among the visitors was Captain George Vancouver, who made three trips. He brought the first cattle and many plants.

In 1820, New England missionaries arrived in the islands. They brought medicines, helped establish laws, courts and schools. They also introduced Mother Hubbards or muumuus as a way of dress for the women.

Iolani Palace

Modern Hawaii

The first legislature was opened by King Kamehameha III in 1845. His throne was covered with a feather war cloak and two large kahili (feather standards) towered over it.

In 1874 King Kalakaua accepted an invitation from the United States government to visit the United States. Queen Liliuokalani, who ruled from 1891 to 1893, was the last Hawaiian monarch. She wrote the words and music to "Aloha Oe" which is played when people arrive and when they leave the islands. She was forced to abdicate and the Republic of Hawaii was formed. Five years later Hawaii was annexed by the United States and in 1900 it became the Territory of Hawaii.

As a territory, Hawaii could elect a delegate to Congress who would represent them but who had no vote. They elected 15 senators and 30 representatives to their own legislature. The president of the United States appointed the governor and other officials.

Hawaii has been an important military base of the United States for many years. Pearl Harbor has grown from a small coaling station to a large installation covering 10,000 acres of land. It is the chief offshore American naval base and was severely damaged in the attack on December 7, 1941. During the Korean War, 3,500 ships were repaired at Pearl Harbor.

Now at Memorial Day services, flags and leis are placed on the graves of veterans who lie buried in National Memorial Cemetery of the Pacific. It is located in shallow Punchbowl Crater and overlooks downtown Honolulu.

Entrance to Hickam Air Force Base

Hawaiian State Flag

During the reign of Kamehameha I, the first Hawaiian flag was designed. Captain Vancouver had presented the king with a British flag which hung outside the royal dwelling for years. The Hawaiian flag was patterned after the English one, with the Union Jack in the upper left corner, but with stripes like the American flag. The present flag of Hawaii was first officially displayed in 1845. The 8 stripes represent the eight principal islands in the Hawaiian group.

For many years Hawaii worked towards statehood. Then in 1947 the House of Representatives approved statehood for Hawaii and passed the bill several times. Finally, in 1959, it was passed by both the House and Senate and was signed by the President. Hawaii is now our 50th state.

Honolulu, the capital city, is the largest of our state capitals in size and one of the largest in population.

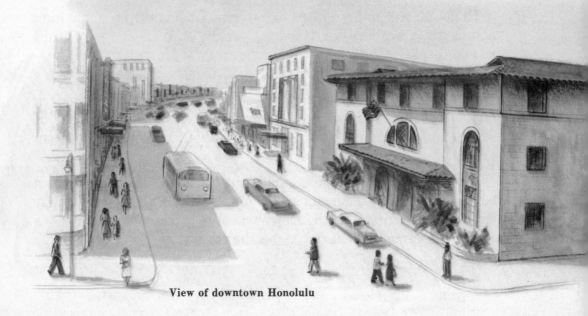

View of downtown Honolulu

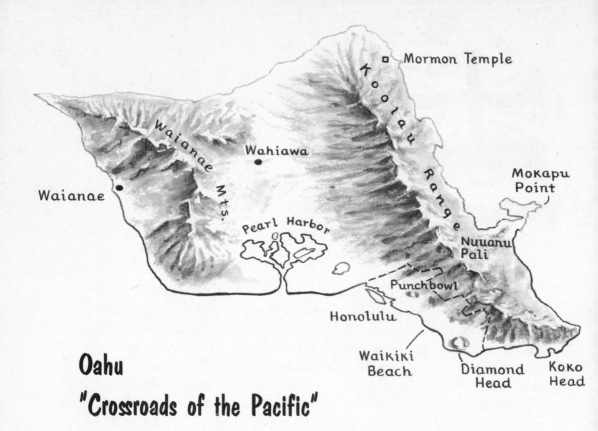

Mormon Temple

Koolau Range

Waianae Mts.

Wahiawa

Mokapu Point

Waianae

Pearl Harbor

Nuuanu Pali

Punchbowl

Honolulu

Waikiki Beach

Diamond Head

Koko Head

Oahu

"Crossroads of the Pacific"

One of the first things you learn in Honolulu is that directions are not given as north and south, east or west. They are given in terms of landmarks. Mauka means towards the mountains, Makai toward the sea.

Honolulu has been called the "crossroads of the Pacific." Most of its supplies come from outside and travel over long distances. Ships and planes stop here on the way to and from Australia and the orient.

Honolulu has many places of interest. It has a fine aquarium, a university and Foster Gardens, where rare trees and shrubs are on display. The Bishop Museum exhibits Hawaiian and Polynesian relics; everything from flutes to feather cloaks.

Although Honolulu has a Polynesian atmosphere, it is a modern city not unlike many of our mainland cities. It has a number of radio and television stations, a symphony orchestra and an academy of arts.

Oahu is the third largest island but the most important and a center of activity. Tourists spend most of their time here. Sugar cane and pineapple are both grown, and in Honolulu there is a pineapple cannery believed to be the largest in the world.

Aloha Tower

Two mountain ranges run along the eastern and western shores of Oahu. The Koolau range catches the trade-winds. It forms a backdrop for the city of Honolulu. The Waianae range includes Oahu's highest peak, Mt. Kaala, 4,030 feet high.

Diamond Head, an extinct volcano, is a landmark famous the world over. Not far away is the Blow Hole, near Koko Crater, a natural hole in the lava ledge through which wave action forces the water up in geysers.

Nuuanu Pali is a 2,000 foot gap in the Koolau mountain range and offers a sweeping view of windward Oahu. A constant wind blows through the pali, often at speeds of 30 to 40 miles an hour. Down the valley, towards Honolulu, these winds are strong enough to force waterfalls upward from the cliffs to form upside down falls.

Many fine beaches ring the island, but the most famous of them all is Waikiki Beach, heart of the islands' tourist industry.

The only Mormon temple outside of continental North America is in Laie. This beautiful temple, built in 1919, is made of cement mixed with lava, yet it gleams like white marble.

Outrigger canoe
at Waikiki Beach

Pineapple
being placed
on conveyor
belts

Pineapple plant
grows two to
four feet high

Sugar and "Pines"

Hawaii's livelihood depends on sugar, pineapples and tourists. Agriculture is highly mechanized and large sums of money are spent for research.

Everyone abbreviates the word pineapple in Hawaii. More than two-thirds of the world's supply of canned "pine" products and an even greater amount of pineapple juice is produced in Hawaii.

Pineapple plants have short, thick stems and from 40 to 50 narrow, sharp pointed leaves. The pineapple "slips" are planted through a mulch paper which helps retain moisture in the soil. It takes 18 to 24 months from planting until the first fruit ripens. At this time, workers go through the fields picking only the fully ripened fruit and placing it on conveyor belts which carry it into trucks. The trucks take it directly to the cannery. Here at the cannery one machine cuts off the ends and removes the core. The fruit then goes into other machines which slice, cut it into chunks or crush it. Pineapple shells are chopped up and dried to make cattle feed.

Pineapple does well in upland areas but sugar cane thrives in the lowlands and was growing on the islands when Captain Cook arrived. Sugar is Hawaii's principal industry.

Sugar cane stands 15 to 20 feet tall. It is a grass which demands plenty of heat, rich soil and water. Irrigation is needed as it takes more than a ton of water to grow a pound of sugar. When the cane ripens it sheds its older, dry leaves around the stalk. Firebreaks are cut out and the cane is burned to get rid of the leaves. At the sugar mill, rollers crush out the juice which is then made into raw sugar, molasses and other products.

Tourists are attracted to Hawaii in ever increasing numbers. About 70 flights per week come into the Honolulu International Airport and there are frequent sailings of large cruise ships to the islands.

Visitors are given a warm welcome and leis to wear. On Lei Day, everybody wears flowers. Pageants are held throughout the islands. Each has a Lei Day queen and court.

There are many other events of interest to tourists. During Aloha Week there are parades, hula and music festivals, luaus and street dancing.

Burning sugar cane

With Spear, Rod and Net

Hawaiians enjoy sport fishing. The natives stand barefooted on lava rocks. They have no weighted nets for idle casting but let their eyes make sure of a successful catch. They also do underwater spear fishing and torch fishing. At Kona, Hawaii, is some of the world's finest deep sea fishing. Kona is famous for catches of marlin, Pacific sailfish and dolphin. Here an 816-pound silver marlin was caught in 1938.

Japanese-American commercial fisherman catch tuna (aku) on barbless hooks with 15-pound live bait. The 30 or more vessels in the tuna fleet seldom go more than 40 miles off shore and they return the same day. Over 5,000 tons of tuna is caught annually.

A hukilau is a community fishing party. A large net is taken out from the beach by boat. Lookouts from nearby hills give the signal when shadows appear, which indicate schools of fish or birds that usually follow them. The net is cast out and pulled back to shore. By custom, any person touching the net can claim a share of the fish.

Spear fisherman

Sea Turtle

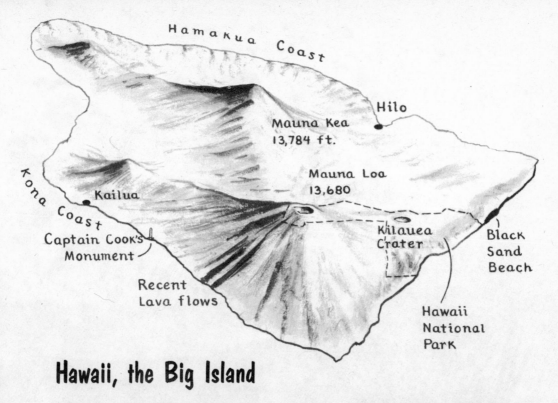

Hamakua Coast

Hilo

Mauna Kea
13,784 ft.

Mauna Loa
13,680

Kona Coast

Kailua

Captain Cook's
Monument

Kilauea
Crater

Black
Sand
Beach

Recent
Lava flows

Hawaii
National
Park

Hawaii, the Big Island

The big island is almost twice as large as the other Hawaiian islands combined. It was formed by five volcanoes. Two of these are still active.

Flying into Hawaii from Oahu, you pass over the wet Hamakua coast, where many waterfalls plunge over cliffs and into the sea.

Hilo is its largest city and the second largest in the islands. Around Hilo are grown large quantities of orchids and anthuriums. Flowers are shipped daily by air-freight to the mainland.

Many cattle are raised on Hawaii. The animals left by the English explorer, Vancouver, ran wild and were roaming around Waimea plateau. The king asked John Parker, a sailor who had left his ship, to round up these cattle for him. Parker stayed on in Hawaii, married an Hawaiian woman and began to build up herds of beef from the wild stock. The Parker Ranch is now one of the largest in the United States.

The Hawaiian cowboy is called paniola. In very dry areas, the cattle strip the thorny covering from the leaf of panini, a form of cactus, and chew the inside to obtain water.

Hawaii National Park extends from the peak of Mauna Loa all the way to the sea. The park contains the largest single mountain mass on earth and the largest active crater in the world. Giant tree ferns grow along the roads into the park.

Pele, Fire Goddess

Hawaii National Park is called the land of Pele, named for the legendary fire goddess who now dwells in Halemaumau, a deep pit within the crater of Kilauea. Steam comes from many lava fissures in and around Kilauea and is piped directly to the steam baths of the volcano house on the brink of the crater.

Kilauea rests on the slope of Mauna Loa, whose oval crater is three miles long. This broad, dome-shaped mountain has been built up by the accumulation of thousands of lava flows.

Mauna Loa erupts about once every three and a half years. Long fissures open up and liquid lava spouts a "curtain of fire" sometimes as high as 800 feet. Debris accumulates to form cinder cones. The lava flows may continue for many weeks and sometimes reach the ocean.

Kilauea and Mauna Loa are among the most active of the world's volcanoes. But they are safe to visit, even during erup-

tions. At the Hawaiian volcano observatory scientists not only study the nature of the two volcanoes but predict eruptions and the course of lava flows.

Pahoehoe (pronounced pahoay-hoay) is a hard, smooth lava usually found in the high, barren regions.

Aa lava — rough
cinder surface

Pahoehoe lava —
smooth surface

Lava flowing
into the sea

Aa (pronounced ah ah) is a soft lava which breaks down rapidly and has made possible the rich soil of the cane fields. When the hot aa (soft lava) flows into the sea, steam explosions throw up lava droplets. These are quickly chilled to form a dark glass and the fragments are then moved by wave action along the shoreline to form beaches of black sand.

Black sand beach

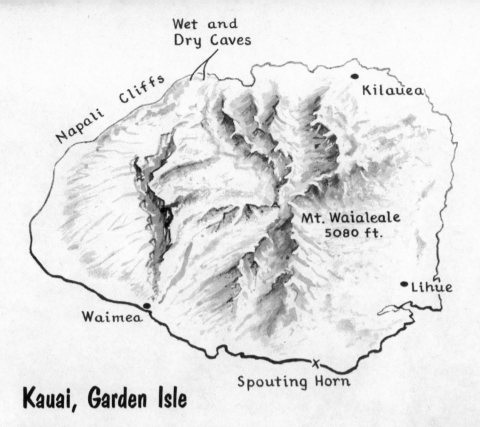

Wet and Dry Caves

Napali Cliffs

Kilauea

Mt. Waialeale
5080 ft.

Lihue

Waimea

X
Spouting Horn

Kauai, Garden Isle

Oldest and most westerly of the islands, Kauai was formed from an ancient volcano. It is 32 miles across. Because of its lush, natural greenery and beautiful gardens, it is called the Garden Isle. Heavy rainfall and a rich soil, originating from volcanic ash, are responsible for this.

For years, Mt. Waialeale, the highest point on the old dome of the volcano, has held the world's record for the highest average rainfall. During more than two decades there has been an average rainfall on Mt. Waialeale of 460 inches, or over 38 feet a year. In 1948, a record 52 feet of rain fell.

The rains have caused erosion of great valleys radiating out from the dome. The deepest valley plunges down over 3,000 feet. Across the island runs a great gash — Waimea Canyon, the "Grand Canyon of the Pacific." Layer upon layer of rock displays dazzling colors, soft blues and greens in the morning and brilliant reds, copper and green in the afternoon. Waimea Canyon is a mile wide at one point, a half mile deep and ten miles long.

Kauai is the most well-watered island of the whole group. Mt. Waialeale's rains supply a hundred waterfalls and send streams rushing down on all sides. The Wailua River is the only navigable fresh waterway in the islands. This river is lined with water hyacinths, beautiful flowering trees and ferns.

Hanapepe Valley — the many waterfalls that are located in this beautiful valley flow from one of the wettest areas on earth.

Sugar cane, which needs plenty of water, has been grown on Kauai since 1835. This island was the first to establish sugar plantations and the first to use locomotives to haul cane from the field to mill. Kauai was also the first to abandon hauling cane by trains. Now thirty-ton trucks transport cane on specially built sixty-foot-wide roads.

Pineapples are also grown on Kauai, and in the lush Hanalei Valley, paddy fields are flooded for rice cultivation. This beautiful valley is known as the "Birthplace of Rainbows."

When the tide and surf are right, the Spouting Horn of Kauai along Koloa Beach will spray a column of water 60 to 100 feet in the air from a hole in the lava rocks. This causes a weird sound which can be heard for miles on calm nights.

Fern Grotto

West of the Spouting Horn is Waimea Bay, where Captain Cook made his historic first landing. Nearby are the remains of an old fort built by the Russians in the early nineteenth century when they wanted to obtain a foothold on Hawaii.

The cliffs of Kauai are spectacular. On the northwest coast, called Napali, the plateau has a sheer drop of about 2,700 feet. Further along the coast are the Wet and Dry Caves of Haena. These were former gathering places of Hawaiian warriors.

Kauai is said to be the island richest in the lore of the menehunes. The menehunes are called the pixies or dwarfs of legendary Hawaii. They were supposedly small people who performed wonderful feats of construction in one night. Anthropologists think they were the original Polynesian settlers. These normal sized people seemed small in comparison to the very tall Polynesian warriors who later came from Tahiti.

Lumahai Beach

Kauai

Molokai

Maui

Niihau

Lanai
City

Lanai

Kahoolawe

Molokai, Lanai, Kahoolawe, Niihau

Three volcanoes built the Island of Molokai. Lack of water has confined industry to growing and canning pineapples and cattle ranching. Fishing at the deep Penguin Bank is the only other source of income. The peninsula of Kalaupapa has a famous leper colony.

Lanai, the pineapple island, is an extinct volcano. In 1922 it was bought by the Hawaiian Pineapple Company and transformed from a semi-wasteland into a great plantation. A town of over 2,500 people was built, consisting almost entirely of company employees and their families.

The heritage of old Hawaii is kept alive on Niihau where probably the largest colony of pure-blooded Hawaiians live. The island has been owned since 1863 by the Scotch family, Robinson, who have protected the Hawaiian way of living by prohibiting visitors. The residents raise sheep, cattle and bees. There are no dogs, telephones, phonographs, automobiles or movies on Niihau. And the Hawaiians here still speak the pure language of their forefathers.

Tiny, uninhabited Kahoolawe Island has been used as a target island for United States warships and Navy and Air Force planes.

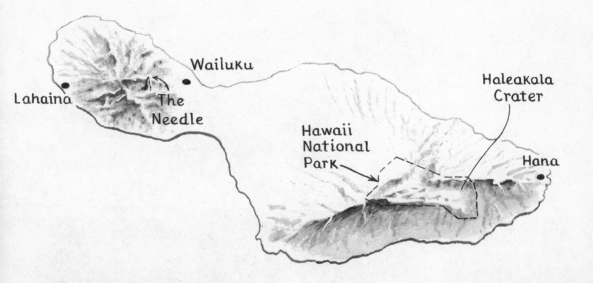

Maui, Sleeping Giant

The Island of Maui was formed by two volcanoes. It is the second largest Hawaiian island, being 25 miles wide one way and 38 the other. On the western end of the island is Mt. Puukukui. This mountain is part of a great volcano which has eroded into the beautiful Iao Valley. In this valley is the Iao Needle, a rock pinnacle, 2,200 feet high, taller than Rio de Janeiro's Sugar Loaf.

The valley between these two volcanoes is a rich plain. Sugar, pineapples and truck crops are grown here by the most modern agricultural methods. Cattle ranches also help support the economy of Maui. Wailuku is the third largest city in Hawaii and the county seat of Maui. It is located at the mouth of the Iao Valley, three miles from Kahului, the principal port.

West of Wailuku is Lahaina, the first white settlement in the Hawaiian Islands. This quiet village was the royal capital of all Hawaii until 1850. Whaling ships anchored here in the nineteenth century and American missionaries founded one of the oldest schools in the United States in this village.

At the opposite end of the island is Haleakala, the world's largest dormant volcano. The top of the crater forms the second part of Hawaii National Park. On the eastern side of Haleakala is Hana Valley, ancient seat of Hawaiian culture. It is a beautiful spot with waterfalls and steep cliffs and a sandy beach. A 10,000-acre cattle ranch is located here.

Haleakala Crater, "House of the Sun"

This is the world's largest dormant volcano. It is seven miles long, two miles wide and ninety miles in circumference at the base. To the top of the crater rim it measures 10,032 feet and the highest cone within the crater is taller than the Empire State Building. Inside the crater grows the rare silversword plant, found only here and on Hawaii. A heavy hair-like growth on the silvery, sword-shaped leaves reflects the sun's rays and helps the plant keep moisture. When the crater is filled with clouds, the shadow of a person standing on the rim is cast on the clouds within a circular rainbow. This is called the Brocken Spectre.